THE SILENT READERS

BY

WILLIAM D. LEWIS, Pd.D., Litt.D.
FORMERLY DEPUTY SUPERINTENDENT, DEPARTMENT OF PUBLIC INSTRUCTION
COMMONWEALTH OF PENNSYLVANIA

ALBERT LINDSAY ROWLAND, A.M., Ph.D.
DIRECTOR BUREAU OF TEACHER TRAINING AND CERTIFICATION, DEPARTMENT OF PUBLIC INSTRUCTION, COMMONWEALTH OF PENNSYLVANIA

AND

ETHEL H. MALTBY GEHRES
CO-AUTHOR OF THE WINSTON READERS

ILLUSTRATED BY
FREDERICK RICHARDSON
AND
EDWIN J. PRITTIE

FIRST READER

THE JOHN C. WINSTON COMPANY

CHICAGO
SAN FRANCISCO

PHILADELPHIA

DALLAS
TORONTO, CAN.

PRINTED IN THE U. S. A. P—4-25

INTRODUCTION

Reading habits. With the recognition of the important place of silent reading in the school has come an appreciation of the necessity of the early development of right reading habits. As soon as the pupil has mastered a small vocabulary, he should be trained to increase his eye-span, shorten his fixations, and follow the line rhythmically. The development of these habits can hardly come too early.

Much of the reading in the first and second grades will, of course, be oral. The danger of mere word-calling, unaccompanied by comprehension of the meaning of the words, is now fully recognized. The danger of slowing down the thought process to the speed of speech is not so generally understood. One may throughout life be handicapped by the habit of reading only as fast as he can pronounce the words even when he is reading silently. This danger alone justifies emphasis on silent reading as soon as pupils have mastered a reading vocabulary of from two to three hundred words.

These dangers will be avoided, and right habits established if the two elements of speed and comprehension are developed. Obviously the development of these factors requires suitable subject matter and treatment carefully adapted to the grade of the pupil.

The purpose of this book. The First Silent Reader aims to provide both material and method for the development of these essential reading habits. Every possible effort has been made to insure not only correct theory, but also practical, workable classroom results. The exercises were worked out with the assistance of experts in primary reading and then printed and tried out in classes under a wide variety of conditions. Extensive revisions to meet the results of these tests insure the practicability and value of this portion of the book.

The selection of subject matter. The subject matter of the First Silent Reader is of two distinct types, material for rapid silent reading, and factual or informational material which must be read carefully and intensively to grasp the meaning.

Extensive rapid silent reading of simple material increases eye-span, shortens fixations, and develops the habit of following lines rhythmically. This type of material is essential to develop speed. However, the exclusive use of rapid reading material may develop speed in reading, with poor comprehension. The material is necessarily simple and does not lend itself to intensive study.

On the other hand, the exclusive use of the factual, informational type of material tends to decrease speed. It must be read slowly and intensively to grasp the entire meaning. Obviously, therefore, a well balanced training in both speed and comprehension requires the two types of material best adapted to develop these two factors. The First Silent Reader contains such a combination, worked out with great care.

Rapid reading material. Story material develops rapid reading. Therefore, most of the rapid reading material in the First Silent Reader consists of the repetitive stories that appeal so strongly to beginners. These stories fix the growing vocabulary by the recurrence of important words. In content they avoid those so frequently used in other readers.

Tests. A wide variety of test and comprehension exercises is given in this book. The directions for carrying out the exercises appear in the pupil's book so that he may early form the habit of interpreting questions and of following printed directions.

Vocabulary. Particular attention has been given to the progressive development of the vocabulary. The vocabulary of the story reappears in the simple test exercises following the selections. The child thus sees the words and phrases in new settings associated with interesting things to do. The conformity of the vocabulary of this book to the Thorndike Word List insures its success with any basal series of readers.

Interleaved manual. The best possible method will be worthless if it is not used. To insure the correct application of the method of this book, an interleaved Manual is provided, which gives complete teaching directions for each page, opposite the page of the pupil's text. The notorious failure of thousands of teachers to make use of the methods carefully prepared by the author is thus obviated.

Method. Provision is made in the Manual for the development of new words. Dramatization, physical and other responses to the printed page, simple tests of various types, inferences, reproduction of story units, and application of information are required. A happy use of the play instinct is made in all of these activities.

Flash cards. The flash cards are words, phrases, and sentences directly related to the material in the readers. They make it possible to give the pupils definite training to increase the eye-span, to develop comprehension, and at the same time drill upon the difficult words and phrases of the story. Their use is carefully explained in the Manual.

Type and illustrations. The type, length of line, and arrangement of the book meet the standards of those who have conducted exhaustive studies of these details. The pictures by Frederick Richardson and Edwin J. Prittie speak for themselves. Four colors are used in all the illustrations.

Acknowledgments. The authors wish to express their sincere appreciation of the assistance they have received from principals, teachers, and supervisors of primary grades. Miss Mary R. Harris, Supervisor of Reading in the Shippensburg Normal School, worked on the manuscript and tested the material from the time the book was begun. Miss Stella Smith and Miss Rena Weider, Reading Specialists of The John C. Winston Company, gave invaluable aid in working on the manuscript and in the tests. Miss Roxanna Steele, formerly Supervisor of Grades in the Bloomsburg Normal School, read the manuscript and gave tests. Among others who tested the tryout edition are Miss Myrtle L. Kaufmann, Supervisor of Grades, Logansport, Indiana; Miss Loretto L. Hoover, Supervisor of Grades, Radnor Township, Pa., and Miss A. J. Megargee, Principal of the Bridesburg Public School, Philadelphia.

CONTENTS

PAGE

"Good-morning!
Polly wants a cracker!"

1. Have you heard a parrot talk?
2. What did the parrot say?
3. Do all birds talk?
4. What can all birds do?

1. What has the little boy in his hand?

2. What will he do with the cracker?

3. What has the little boy under his arm?

4. Where is he going?

5. What will he do with the book?

6. Can Polly read the book?

---

1. The little boy can talk.
2. The little boy can read.
3. Polly can ______.
4. Polly can not ______.
5. All birds can ______.
6. Not all birds can ______.

DO YOU KNOW?

1. Who says, "Moo-moo"?
2. Who says, "Quack-quack"?
3. Who says, "Bow-wow"?
4. Who says, "Peep-peep"?
5. Who says, "Polly wants a cracker"?
6. Who says, "Meow-meow"?

1. What does the hen say?
2. What does the rooster say?
3. What does the duck say?
4. What does the little chick say?
5. What does the goose say?
6. What does the owl say?
7. What does the turkey say?
8. What does the parrot say?

---

1. What does the cat say?
2. What does the dog say?
3. What does the cow say?
4. What does the sheep say?
5. What does the pig say?

CAN YOU TELL?

One day a man was standing
on the street.
He was selling something.
In his hand
were many round things.
He held them by strings.
Some of them were red.
Some of them were blue.
And some were yellow.
Once the man let go
of a string.
Then something red
went up, up into the sky.
It never came back again.
Can you tell
what the man was selling?

MAKING BALLOONS

Your teacher will give you some crayons.

She will give you some paper.

---

1. Find the red crayon.
2. Hold up the red crayon.
3. Draw a red balloon.
4. Put the red crayon on your desk.

---

1. Find the blue crayon.
2. Hold up the blue crayon.
3. Draw a blue balloon.
4. Put the blue crayon on your desk.

1. Hold up
the yellow crayon.

2. Draw a yellow balloon.

3. Put the yellow crayon
on your desk.

---

1. Hold up the black crayon.

2. Draw black strings
on the balloons.

3. Put the black crayon
on your desk.

---

1. Turn over your paper.

2. Draw a balloon-man.

3. Draw a red balloon
in his hand.

4. Draw a blue balloon
in his hand.

5. Draw two yellow balloons
in his hand.

A BIRTHDAY CAKE

(WHEN SOME ONE HAS A BIRTHDAY)

To-day is______ birthday.

How old is______?

Please stand,______.

Who will wish______
a happy birthday?

Let us make a cake for_____.

We can make it
on the blackboard.

1. Who can draw a cake
on the blackboard?

2. How many candles
do we need?

3. Who will make
a red candle?

4. Who will make
a blue candle?

5. Who will make
a yellow candle?

6. How many more candles
do we need?

7. Who will make
these candles?

1. How can we light the candles?

2. Who will light a blue candle?

3. Who will light a red candle?

4. Who will light a yellow candle?

5. How many more candles are on the cake?

6. Who will light these candles?

---

1. How can we blow out the candles?

2. We will let ______ blow out the candles.

1. Where are the children playing?

What do you think they are doing?

1. Give the boy a name.
2. Give the girl a name.
3. Name the girl's toys.
4. Name the boy's toys.
5. What happened to the train?

---

1. How many dolls do you see?
2. What are the dolls doing?

---

1. What will the boy do with the ball?
2. What will happen to the soldiers?
3. Do you like to read about soldiers?
4. Soon you will read about a lead soldier.

THE LEAD SOLDIER

Once upon a time there was a box of lead soldiers.

One soldier said,
"I think I will march away
to see the world."

So this lead soldier
marched away.

1. Can you stand
like the lead soldier?
2. Can you march
like the lead soldier?
3. If you can,
raise your hand.

HE MEETS THE RAG DOLL

Soon the lead soldier
met a rag doll.
"Halt!" said the lead soldier.
The rag doll stood still.

"Who are you?"
asked the lead soldier.

"I am a rag doll,"
said the rag doll.

"Are you a friend?"
asked the lead soldier.

"I am a friend
to every one,"
said the rag doll.

"Then you may go on,"
said the lead soldier.
So they both went on.

1. Whom did the lead soldier meet first?
2. What did he ask her?
3. What did the rag doll say?
4. Then what did they both do?

Then the lead soldier
went on and on.
Soon he met a tin horse.

"Halt!" said the lead soldier.
The tin horse stood still.
"Who are you?"
asked the lead soldier.

'I am a tin horse,"
said the tin horse.

"Are you a friend?"
asked the lead soldier.

"I am a friend
to every one,"
said the tin horse.

"Then you may go on," said the lead soldier.

So they both went on.

1. Whom did the lead soldier meet next?

2. Do you remember what the lead soldier said to the tin horse?

3. Do you remember what the tin horse said to the lead soldier?

4. Can you tell this part of the story?

5. Perhaps your teacher will let you play this part of the story.

HE MEETS THE WOOLLY DOG

Then the lead soldier
met a woolly dog.
"Halt!" said the lead soldier.
The woolly dog stood still.
"Who are you?"
asked the lead soldier.

"I am a woolly dog,"
said the woolly dog.

"Are you a friend?"
asked the lead soldier.

"I am a friend
to every one,"
said the woolly dog.

"Then you may go on,"
said the lead soldier.
So they both went on.

1. Let us play
this part of the story.
2. What does a dog do?
3. Can you be a woolly dog?
4. If you can,
raise your hand.
5. Choose a friend
to be the lead soldier.
6. Lead soldier and woolly dog,
begin to play.

HE MEETS THE PAPER LION

Soon the lead soldier
met a paper lion.
"Halt!" said the lead soldier.
The paper lion stood still.

"Who are you?"
asked the lead soldier.

"I am the paper lion,"
said the paper lion.

"Are you a friend?"
asked the lead soldier.

"No! I am not your friend,"
said the paper lion.

And the lion roared.

Then the lead soldier said,
"You are not my friend?
Then I will fight you."

"Very well," said the lion.

So the soldier and the lion
began to fight.

The paper lion
began to tear. Soon he was
all torn to pieces.

Then the lead soldier
went back to his box.

1. What happened
to the paper lion?
2. Can you act like the lion?
3. If you can, raise your hand.
4. Choose a friend
to be the lead soldier.
5. Lead soldier and paper lion,
begin to play.

MAKING OTHERS HAPPY

PLAYING A STORY

Children in the kindergarten like to see little plays.

They do not know the story of "The Lead Soldier."

Let us play it for them.

1. Who can name the players in the story?
2. Who can be a good lead soldier?
3. If you think you can, raise your hand.
4. The lead soldier may choose

   a rag doll
   a tin horse
   a woolly dog
   and a paper lion.

Where will
the lead soldier's box be?
Where will the world be?

---

1. Where did the soldier live?
2. Why did he march away?
3. Whom did he meet first?
4. Was she a friend?
5. How many players are in this part of the story?
6. Play this part of the story.

---

1. Whom did the soldier meet next?
2. Was he a friend?
3. How many players are in this part of the story?
4. Play this part of the story.

1. Whom did the soldier meet after the tin horse?

2. What did he say to it?

3. What did the woolly dog say?

4. Name the players in this part of the story.

5. Play this part of the story.

---

1. Whom did the soldier meet last of all?

2. Was this a friend?

3. How many players in this part of the story?

4. Play this part of the story.

Now play all of the story.

Then we can play it for the kindergarten children.

PUZZLES

Here are some puzzles.

There are some words left out on this page.

Can you tell what they are?

Can you read the page?

---

1. First the lead soldier met a _____ doll.
2. Then he _____ a tin horse.
3. The lead_____ met a_____dog.
4. The _____ soldier met a _____ lion.
5. The paper lion began to _____ to pieces.
6. The _____ soldier went back to his _____.

MAKING PAPER SOLDIERS

You will need some crayons.

Your teacher will give you a sheet of thin paper.

Draw or trace four soldiers in a row.

1. Write the number 1 under the first soldier.

2. Write the number 2 under the next soldier.

3. Write the number 3 under the next soldier.

4. Write the number 4 under the last soldier.

---

1. Find soldier number 3.
2. Color him blue.
3. Find soldier number 1.
4. Color him red.
5. Find soldier number 2.
6. Color him black.
7. Find soldier number 4.
8. Color him blue and red.

Can you cut out your soldiers?

THE SPARROW AND THE BLADE OF GRASS

Once a sparrow
sat on a blade of grass.
She said to it,
"Give me a swing,
blade of grass."

But the blade of grass said, "No, I will not."

So the sparrow flew off to the goat. She said to him, "Mr. Goat, Mr. Goat, go and eat the blade of grass, because it will not give me a swing."

But the goat answered, "No, I will not."

1. What did the sparrow ask the blade of grass?
2. Why did the sparrow fly to Mr. Goat?
3. What did the goat say?

So the sparrow
flew off to the wolf.

She said to him,
"Mr. Wolf, Mr. Wolf,
go and eat the goat,
because he will not go
and eat the blade of grass,
and the blade of grass
will not give me a swing."

But the wolf answered,
"No, I will not."

1. Whom did the sparrow fly to next?
2. What did Mr. Wolf say?

SHE FLIES TO MR. MAN

So the sparrow flew off to a man.

She said to him,

"Mr. Man, Mr. Man,

go and kill the wolf,
because he will not go
and eat the goat,
and the goat will not go
and eat the blade of grass,
and the blade of grass
will not give me a swing."

But the man answered,
"No, I will not."

1. What did the sparrow do in this part of the story?

2. Is it easy for a man to kill a wolf?

3. How many has the sparrow talked to?

SHE FLIES TO THE FIRE

So the sparrow flew off to the fire.

She said to it,
"Fire, fire,
go and burn the man,
because he will not go
and kill the wolf,
and the wolf will not go
and eat the goat,
and the goat will not go
and eat the blade of grass,
and the blade of grass
will not give me a swing."

But the fire answered,
"No, I will not."

1. What did the sparrow tell the fire to do?
2. What did the fire answer?

So she flew to the water.
She said to it, "Water, water, go and put out the fire, because it will not go and burn the man, and the man will not go and kill the wolf, and the wolf will not go and eat the goat, and the goat will not go and eat the blade of grass, and the blade of grass will not give me a swing."

But the water answered, "No, I will not."

> Why did the sparrow fly to the water?

So the sparrow flew off to the ox.

She said to him,
"Ox, ox,
go and drink up the water,
because it will not go
and put out the fire,
and the fire will not go
and burn the man,
and the man will not go
and kill the wolf,
and the wolf will not go
and eat the goat,
and the goat will not go
and eat the blade of grass,
and the blade of grass
will not give me a swing."

Then the ox went off
to drink the water,
and the water went off
to put out the fire,
and the fire went off
to burn the man,
and the man went off
to kill the wolf,
and the wolf went off
to eat the goat,
and the goat went off
to eat the blade of grass,
and the blade of grass
had a terrible fright.

Then the blade of grass
began to swing the sparrow
and sing,

"Hush-a-bye, baby,
on the tree top,
You had better hold tight,
if not, you will drop."

1. Who helped the sparrow first?

2. Who helped the sparrow next?

3. Name all who helped the sparrow.

4. What did the blade of grass sing?

FINDING WORDS

Can you read these words?

swing	man	grass
goat	fire	ox
wolf	water	sparrow

---

1. Find the name of a bird.

2. Find the name of something green.

3. Find the name of something hot.

4. Find the name of something wet.

5. Find the name of something which flies.

6. Find the names of all the animals.

DRESSING DOLLS

Do you remember the rag doll in the story of "The Lead Soldier"?

Let us dress some dolls.

Draw or trace three dolls in a row.

1. Find the doll in the middle.
2. Color her dress red.
3. Color her hair black.
4. Color her stockings brown.

---

1. Find the doll on the right.
2. Color her dress blue.
3. Color her hair brown.
4. Color her stockings black.

---

1. Find the doll on the left.
2. Choose a color for her dress.
3. Color her hair black.
4. Choose a color for her stockings.

MOTHER GOOSE'S CHILDREN

Can you tell their names?

1. Who sat in a corner?

2. Who jumped over the candlestick?

3. Who fell from a wall?

4. Who went up the hill to get some water?

5. Who went to sleep under a haystack?

6. Who met a pieman?

7. Who lost her sheep?

8. Who went
to the cupboard?

9. Who sat on a tuffet?

---

1. Choose a number.

2. Be ready to play it.

3. When you are ready
raise your hand.

You will need
paper and pencil.

1. Draw a picture
of number 2.

2. Draw a picture
of number 5.

3. Choose a number
and draw the picture.

We will try to tell
the number of your picture.

This is a picture
of Fairy Good Health.

She is writing a letter
to you.

FAIRY GOOD HEALTH'S LETTER

Dear Boys and Girls:

Do all you boys and girls want to be well and strong?

If you do, you must drink milk and eat fruit.

Do not eat much candy.

Always brush your teeth after you eat.

Brush your teeth when you go to bed, too.

Always go to bed early.

Open your windows when you go to bed.

Love to you all,

FAIRY GOOD HEALTH.

A LETTER TO FAIRY GOOD HEALTH

Can you read
Fairy Good Health's letter?

1. What did she tell you to eat?

2. What did she tell you to drink?

3. What did she say about brushing your teeth?

4. What did she say about going to bed?

Would you like to answer Fairy Good Health's letter?

Your teacher will write the letter for you.

Tell her what to write.

Tell Fairy Good Health what you will try to do.

THINGS TO DRAW

Let us make some pictures for Fairy Good Health.

We can send them to her.

We shall need paper, pencils, and crayons.

---

1. Draw an orange
in the middle of the paper.
2. Color the orange.
3. Draw an apple
at the right of the orange.
4. Color the apple red.
5. Draw a banana at the left of the orange.
6. Color the banana.

Can you think of some things to draw?

A TEA PARTY

Come on, Betty Jane,
play tea party with me.
Let's set the table
out under the tree.
That cup is yours,
and this one is mine,
Here are the saucers—
now isn't that fine?

The sugar bowl's empty,
 we'll play there's some there.
The cream is just water,
 but what do we care?
And mother will give us
 some milk for the tea,
She says it is better
 for you and for me.

Now I'll run to the kitchen
 and get the surprise.
I can't tell you what,
 but you'll open your eyes.
You never can guess,
 guess hard as you can—
Mother's just baked
 a big Gingerbread Man!

—*Anne Gage.*

1. Who invited Betty to the tea party?

2. Where did they have the tea party?

3. What was in the sugar bowl?

4. What did they have for cream?

5. What did they have for tea?

---

1. Find the words which tell where they had the party.

2. Find the words which tell what the surprise was.

3. Find the word which tells who made the surprise.

Who can draw a Gingerbread Man on the blackboard?

1. Who is this?

2. What did the fairy say about milk?

3. Do you like milk?

4. What does the milkman do when it rains or snows?

5. Can you name some people who need no milkman?

1. How can you tell when a fire truck is coming?

2. What should you do when a fire truck comes along?

3. Why is a fireman as brave as a soldier?

1. Who is this?

2. Why is a policeman called "the children's friend"?

3. How does he help your fathers and mothers?

4. What does a policeman do to the people who do not obey him?

1. Who is this?
2. What has he in his bag?
3. Did the mailman ever bring a letter to you?
4. Who wrote your letter?

5. Where does the mailman get his letters?

6. How does he know where to take the letters?

7. How can we help the mailman?

Let us play mailman.

Read the little play silently.

When you are ready to play, raise your hand.

1. Put the letters in your bag.
2. Put the bag on your back.
3. Walk along the street.
4. Take a letter out of your bag.
5. Read the name.
6. Put the letter in a mail box.

DO YOU KNOW?

1. Who brings milk to your house?
2. Who brings bread to your house?
3. Who puts out the fire in burning houses?
4. Who is called "the children's friend"?
5. Who brings your letters?
6. Who helps the children to cross the street?
7. Who brings your coal?
8. Who brings ice to your house?
9. Who takes away your ashes?
10. Who brings meat to your house?

PLAYING RADIO

Have you ever heard a story over the radio?

Who told the story?

Let us play telling the story of "The Three Bears" over the radio.

How many players shall we need?

Who can choose a good story-teller?

Who can choose some one to tell what the story will be?

Who would like to listen?

What will you put on your ears?

1. Who is the little girl?

2. How many bowls do you see?

3. How many chairs do you see?

4. What will the little girl do first?

5. What will she do next?

6. Then where will she go?

1. What are the names of the bears?

2. Why did the bears come home?

3. What did each bear say?

4. Why did they go upstairs?

5. What did they find there?

6. Where was the little girl?

7. How does the story end?

PLAYING THE THREE BEARS

Let us play
we are Goldenhair.

Who can:

1. Rap on the bears' door?
2. Eat the porridge?
3. Sit in the chairs?
4. Go to sleep?

Let us all be bears.

Who can:

1. Walk like a bear?
2. Talk like the little bear?
3. Talk like the big bear?
4. Eat hot porridge?
5. Find Goldenhair in bed?

GOING TO THE MOVIES

1. Where are the children going?

2. Who are taking them?

3. What is the name of the picture?

4. Where do they buy their tickets?

5. What do they do with their tickets?

PLAYING MOVIES

Let us play movies.

Where shall our theater be?

Let us play
"The Three Bears."

How will people know what picture they are going to see?

Let us make some pictures for the outside of our theater.

Take paper and crayons.

---

1. Draw Goldenhair.
2. Color her dress red.
3. Color her stockings black.
4. What color was her hair?

1. Draw the three bears in the woods.
2. Color the bears.
3. Color the trees green.

1. Draw the bears' table.
2. Draw three bowls
on the table.
3. Color the bowls yellow.
4. Can you
make the porridge hot?

1. Draw three chairs
near the table.
2. Choose a color
for the chairs.
3. Color the chairs.

Can you make
other pictures of the bears?

We will put the best pictures
outside of the theater.

Then people will know
what they are going to see.

Now we are ready to play.

1. How many players do we need?

2. Who will sell tickets?

3. Where will you sell the tickets?

4. Who will take the tickets?

5. Where will you take the tickets?

The other children may come to see the picture.

You may buy your tickets.

Give your tickets to the man at the door.

Take your seats in the theater.

Players, begin the movie.

PLAYING SENTENCES

Read these sentences to yourself.

Be ready to play them.

1. The lead soldier marched away.
2. The woolly dog barked.
3. The paper lion roared.
4. The sparrow flew away.
5. Fairy Good Health wrote a letter.
6. The policeman held up his hand.
7. The mailman put a letter in the box.
8. The fireman drove the fire truck.

1. What are the children doing?

2. How many pets are in the picture?

3. How many of the pets can run?

4. How many of the pets can hop?

5. How many of the pets have wings?

1. What does the dog like to eat?

2. What does the cat eat?

3. Do you know what a hen eats?

4. What do the chicks eat?

5. What do these pets drink?

---

1. Which pets are the children feeding?

2. What are the children feeding the rabbits?

3. What other food do rabbits like to eat?

4. You are going to read a story about five little rabbits.

5. What do you think they ate?

THE LITTLE OLD WOMAN AND MRS. RABBIT

Once upon a time
a little old woman
had a garden.

She had lettuce,
cabbage, and carrots
in her garden.

One day Mrs. Rabbit came to the garden. She began to take some lettuce.

The little old woman called to Mrs. Rabbit, "Go away, rabbit! Do not take my lettuce, or I will throw a stone at you."

Mrs. Rabbit said, "Come home with me. Then you will see why I need your lettuce."

But the little old woman said, "No, I will not go home with you."

So she threw a stone
at Mrs. Rabbit.

Mrs. Rabbit hopped away.

1. What was Mrs. Rabbit doing in the garden?
2. What did the little old woman say?
3. What did Mrs. Rabbit say?
4. What did the little old woman do to Mrs. Rabbit?

The next day Mrs. Rabbit came again to the garden. She began to take some of the carrots.

The little old woman came out of her home. She called to Mrs. Rabbit, "Go away, rabbit! Do not take my carrots, or I will throw a stone at you."

Mrs. Rabbit said, "Do not throw a stone at me. Come home with me.

Then you will see
why I need your carrots,
and you will not
throw a stone at me."

The little old woman said,
"No, I will not
go home with you."
So she threw a stone
at Mrs. Rabbit.

Mrs. Rabbit
hopped away
to her home again.

Let us play
this part of the story.
1. Who can be
the little old woman?
2. Who can be Mrs. Rabbit?

The next day
Mrs. Rabbit came again
to the old woman's garden.

She began
to take some cabbage.

The little old woman
called to Mrs. Rabbit,
"Go away, rabbit!
Do not take my cabbage,
or I will throw a stone
at you."

Mrs. Rabbit said,
"Please come home with me.
Then you will see
why I need your cabbage."

This time
the little old woman
went with Mrs. Rabbit.

Soon they came
to Mrs. Rabbit's home.
There they saw
five baby rabbits.

All the baby rabbits
were eating.
Some were eating lettuce.
Some were eating carrots.

The little old woman smiled, and said,

"Your little rabbits may have all the carrots and lettuce and cabbage they need."

So Mrs. Rabbit went to the garden every day.

The little old woman never threw a stone again.

1. How many times did Mrs. Rabbit go to the garden?
2. How many times did the little old woman throw stones?
3. Why did the little old woman stop throwing stones?

Here is a picture
of the players
in the story of
"The Little Old Woman
and Mrs. Rabbit."

How many players
are there?

What are their names?

1. Who can be Mrs. Rabbit?

2. Who can be the little old woman?

3. Mrs. Rabbit may choose the five little rabbits.

---

1. What did Mrs. Rabbit take from the garden first?

2. What did she take next?

3. What did she take last?

4. When did the little old woman go to Mrs. Rabbit's house?

5. What did she say then?

Mrs. Rabbit, take your rabbits home.

Then begin to play the story.

FOOD FOR THE RABBITS

You will need paper, pencil, crayons, or paints.

Draw Mrs. Rabbit and her five baby rabbits.

What did Mrs. Rabbit give her rabbits to eat?

1. Draw a carrot for each rabbit.
2. How many carrots did you draw?
3. Color the carrots.

---

1. Draw a cabbage for each baby rabbit and one for Mrs. Rabbit.
2. How many cabbages did you draw?
3. Color the cabbages.

THE DAYS OF THE WEEK

Here are the names
of the days in a week:

Sunday
Monday
Tuesday
Wednesday
Thursday
Friday
Saturday

How many days are there?

What is the day
after Sunday?
What is the day
before Friday?

What is the day
before Saturday?

What is the day
after Monday?

What is the day
before Sunday?

What is the day
before Wednesday?

What is the day
after Friday?

What is the day
before Monday?

What is the day
after Wednesday?

What day is to-day?
What day was yesterday?
What day will to-morrow be?

1. What are the names of the school days?

2. What days are not school days?

Draw a picture of something you like to do on Saturdays.

MAKING UP STORIES

You know how
to play stories.

You know how
to read stories.

Do you know how
to make up stories?

Can you make up a story
about a little girl who
was lost and was found again?

When you are ready
to tell your story,
raise your hand.

Your teacher will write
the best stories on the board.

Make up a story
about a hen
and her little chicks.

Make up a story
about a cat
and a cross dog.

Make up a story
about a balloon
on a windy day.

Make up a story
about some boys
and a football.

Make up a story
about Santa Claus
and the three bears' stockings.

AT THE SEA SHORE

1. Where are the children playing?

2. What season is it?

3. Why do people go to the sea shore?

4. Do you like to go to the sea shore?

1. How many children are in the picture?

2. How many are boys?

3. How many are girls?

4. What is the man doing?

5. What are the ladies doing?

---

1. How many ponies do you see?

2. Why does the man walk with the pony?

3. Who is riding the other pony?

4. How can you tell that he is a good rider?

5. What else do children do at the sea shore?

THE SEASONS

There are four seasons in a year.

The seasons are:

spring	summer
fall	winter

In the spring, the birds come back.

The trees get new leaves.

We plant our gardens in the spring.

In the summer, the weather is warm.

The flowers are in bloom.
We go to the sea shore.

In the fall,
the nuts are ripe.
Jack Frost
paints the leaves.

In the winter,
the birds go South.
Then the snow comes.

---

1. How many seasons are there?
2. How do we know when it is spring?
3. How do we know when it is summer?
4. When does Jack Frost paint the leaves?
5. When do the birds fly South?

1. Who is this?

2. What is he going to do?

3. What season is it?

4. What will happen to the leaves?

CAN YOU TELL?

1. What season do we have before the fall?

2. What season do we have after the fall?

3. What season do we have after the winter?

4. What season do we have after the summer?

---

1. What do you like to do in the fall?

2. What do you like to do in the spring?

3. Tell two things you like to do in summer.

4. Tell three things you like to do in winter.

PICTURES TO DRAW ON THE BLACKBOARD

1. Draw a boy
flying a kite.

2. Draw a girl
picking flowers.

3. Draw some leaves
falling from a tree.

4. Draw a boy
pulling a sled.

Who can find
a winter picture?

Who can find
a summer picture?

Who can find a fall picture?

Who can find
a spring picture?

OUR SNOW-MAN

Let us make a snow-man on the board.

1. Who can draw his body?
2. Who can draw his head?
3. Who can draw his eyes?
4. Who will put on his ears?
5. Who will make his nose?
6. Who will draw his mouth?
7. Who will put a hat on his head?

---

1. What does the sun do to a snow-man?
2. How can we melt our snow-man?
3. Who will be the sun and melt our snow-man?

Our Fred and Flo
Took piles of snow
To make a great big
Snow-Man.
They worked all day,
But it was play.
Just see their funny
Snow-Man!

But Mr. Sun
Thought it was fun
To shine upon their Snow-Man.
And then, alas,
It came to pass
They had a melting Snow-Man.

—Margaret Ford.

BLACK CAT'S BELL

Once upon a time
Gray Mouse had some cheese.

Black Cat saw Gray Mouse.

Gray Mouse
did not eat his cheese.
He was frightened.

Black Cat ran after him,
but she could not catch him.

1. Who frightened Gray Mouse?
2. What did Gray Mouse do with the cheese?
3. How did Gray Mouse get away from Black Cat?

GRAY MOUSE CALLS HIS FRIENDS

Gray Mouse called his friends.

His friends were Thin Tail, Long Nose, and Sharp Ears.

They were all afraid of Black Cat.

Gray Mouse said, "How can we keep away from Black Cat?"

"I do not know. She makes no noise," said Sharp Ears.

"She has sharp claws," said Thin Tail.

"She can smell mice,"
said Long Nose.

1. How many friends did Gray Mouse have?
2. What were their names?
3. What did Gray Mouse ask his friends?

GRAY MOUSE'S PLAN

"I have a plan,"
said Gray Mouse.

"What is your plan?"
asked the mice.

"Tie a bell
on Black Cat's neck,"
said Gray Mouse.
"Then we shall know
when Black Cat is coming.
We shall hear the bell.

What do you think
of my plan?" said Gray Mouse.

"I think that your plan
is a good plan," said Thin Tail.

"I think that
it is a good plan,"
said Sharp Ears.

"I think that
it is a good plan,"
said Long Nose.

Gray Mouse was happy.
All the mice were happy.

1. What was Gray Mouse's plan?
2. What did the mice think of the plan?
3. What do you think of the plan?

WAS IT A GOOD PLAN?

Then Gray Mouse said,
"Who will tie a bell
on Black Cat's neck?"

All the mice were still.
They did not know
what to say to Gray Mouse.

Then Gray Mouse said,
"Thin Tail,
you must tie the bell
on Black Cat's neck."

But Thin Tail said,
"Oh no! I can not tie a bell
on Black Cat's neck.
You must do it."

Gray Mouse said,
"I can not tie a bell
on Black Cat's neck.
Long Nose, you must
tie the bell
on Black Cat's neck."

Long Nose said,
"Oh no! I can not
tie a bell
on Black Cat's neck.
Let Sharp Ears do it."

But Sharp Ears said,
"Oh no! I can not tie a bell
on Black Cat's neck."

There was no one
who would tie a bell
on Black Cat's neck.

Then all the mice
went home.

And a bell never was
tied on Black Cat's neck.

1. What was the matter with Gray Mouse's plan?
2. How does the story end?

A LITTLE PLAY

Let us play the story about Black Cat's Bell.

How many players do we need?

What are their names?

Who can be Black Cat?

Who can be Gray Mouse?

How many friends did Gray Mouse have?

What were their names?

Gray Mouse, you may choose your friends.

How many players do we need for the first page?

When do we need the other players?

Begin to play.

MAKING A PICTURE BOOK

Would you like to make a little picture book?

You will need paper and pencil.

You will need something to tie your book together.

Can you think of something you can use to tie your book together?

---

1. Draw a picture of Gray Mouse.

2. Draw a picture of Gray Mouse's cheese.

3. Draw Black Cat running after Gray Mouse.

1. Draw Gray Mouse
in the middle
of a piece of paper.

2. Draw Thin Tail
at the left
of Gray Mouse.

3. Draw Long Nose
near Thin Tail.

4. Draw Sharp Ears
at the right
of Gray Mouse.

5. Draw the bell
near Gray Mouse.

6. Put a red string
on the bell.

Tie your book together.

What name will you
give your book?

FAIRIES

Can you remember a story about a fairy?

Who was the fairy who wrote a letter to you?

Do you remember what she said in her letter?

What did you send to her?

You are going to read about another fairy to-day.

This fairy likes children who have good manners.

Let us play that she has come to see us to-day.

This is a picture
of Fairy Good Manners.

What has she
in her hand?

When she sees children
who have good manners,
she waves her wand at them.

PLAYING FAIRY

Who will choose some one to be Fairy Good Manners?

What may she have for a wand?

If you have good manners, what will Fairy Good Manners do?

Read the questions.

If you know the answers, raise your hand.

1. What should you say when you walk in front of people?

2. What should you say when a friend has a birthday?

3. What should you say when you leave a party?

4. What should you say when you ask for something?

5. What should you say when you are given something?

6. What should a boy do when he meets a lady on the street?

7. What should you do when older people come into the room?

8. What should you do when others are talking?

Please stand, if the fairy waved her wand at you.

1. Who is the little girl?

2. Where is she going?

3. What has she in her basket?

4. What did her mother tell her to do?

5. What did the little girl tell the wolf?

6. What did the wolf plan to do?

The wolf got to Grandmother's house first

But Grandmother had gone for some water.

1. Who did the little girl think was in the bed?

2. What did she say?

3. How did the wolf answer?

4. Who saved the little girl from the wolf?

USING THE TELEPHONE

1. When you want
to telephone,
what do you do first?

2. How do you
call the number?

3. What should you say
when it is time to stop?

4. What do you do
when Central gives you
the wrong number?

5. What do you do
when some one is talking
on the line?

6. Have you a telephone
at your house?

TELEPHONING OUR FRIENDS

Here are three plays.
Read the first one.
When you are ready to play, raise your hand.

1. Call up a girl friend.

Ask her to come to your house to play with you.

Your teacher will choose two girls to play.

She will choose one girl to call up.

What will the other girl do?

Girls, begin to play!

Read the next play.

When you are ready to play it, raise your hand.

2. Call up a boy friend.

Ask him to play ball with you after school.

Some one will choose
two boys to play.
Boys, begin to play!

Read the next play.
When you are ready to play,
raise your hand.

> 3. Call up a friend.
> Play that the line is busy.
> Call up again.
> Tell your friend
> that you are not going
> to school to-day.

Your teacher will choose
two children to play.
Begin to play!

A HAPPY FAMILY

Here are some questions about this picture.

Read each question.

Find the answers in the picture.

1. How many are there in this family?

2. How many children are there?

3. Which meal are they going to eat?

4. How do you know?

5. To whom is the mother speaking?

6. Why do you think so?

7. What do you think she is saying?

8. Who is the dog's best friend?

9. Why must the dog be sent out of the room?

10. What is the father doing?

11. Why are the flowers on the table?

12. Why is this a happy family?

OUR FLAG

1. Where is the red on the flag?
2. Where is the white on the flag?
3. Can you find the blue?
4. When do we see the flag on our schoolhouse?
5. When do we put out our flags?
6. When should we take in our flags?
7. Can you name some days when our flag should be out?
8. Do you know a song about our flag?

1. Your teacher will ask a boy to hold the flag.

2. She will ask you all to salute the flag.

3. Salute the flag!

How many red stripes are in the flag?

How many white stripes are in the flag?

How many can make a flag?

You will need some paper and some crayons.

Draw a large flag.

Where will the red be?

What will you make blue?

How can you make the stars?

A THINKING GAME

Did you ever play
a thinking game?

Can you tell the names of
these birds and animals?

1. I am thinking
of an animal.
It lives in trees and eats nuts.
What is it?

2. I am thinking of a bird.
It is black, white, and red.
Its head is red.
It has a long bill.
It taps on trees.
What is it?

3. I am thinking of an animal.
It lives in houses.
It has soft feet.
It drinks milk.
What is it?

4. I am thinking of another animal.
It has a short tail.
It has long ears.
What is it?

5. I am thinking of a bird.
It is red and green and yellow.
It likes crackers.
It can talk.
What is it?

THE CAT, THE COCK, AND THE FOX

Once upon a time
a cat and a cock
lived on a farm.

One day the farmer
scolded the cock.

He said,
"Do not crow so loudly."

Then the cock
was not happy.

He wanted to crow loudly.

So he said to the cat,
"Let us go to the woods
and live together."

"Very well," said the cat. "Let us go to the woods and live together."

So they built a house in the woods.

There they lived together.

1. Why did the farmer scold the cock?

2. Why did the cat and the cock build a house?

One day the cat went out to find something to eat.

A sly fox saw him go.

He said to himself, "There goes the cat! Now I will get the cock."

The fox went to the house. He sang,
"Little cock, little cock,
Come with me for a walk."

The cock came out.

The fox caught him and ran off with him.

But the cock cried,
"Help, pussy, help!
The fox holds me tight
with all his might!

Help, pussy, help!"

The cat heard the cock cry, and ran after the fox.

When the fox saw the cat, he let the cock go.

1. Why did the cat leave the cock all alone?

2. What happened to the cock?

The next day
when the cat went away,
the fox came again.

He sang,
"Little cock, little cock,
Come with me for a walk."

"Oh no," said the cock,
"I will not go with you."

"But," the fox said,
"I will give you some corn."

The cock wanted some corn.
But he said, "I will not go.
The cat told me
not to open the door."

Soon the fox sang again.
This time the cock
opened the door.

Then the fox caught him and ran off with him.

But the cock cried,
"Help, pussy, help!
The fox holds me tight
with all his might!
Help, pussy, help!"

The cat heard him,
but he could not catch the fox.

The fox put the cock in a bag.

He said, "You stay there until dinner time."

1. Why did the cock open the door again?
2. What had the cat told him to do?

THE CAT'S TRICK

The cat went home.
He cried and cried
because the fox
had caught the cock.
Then he got a fiddle
and a bag.

He went to the fox's house.

He began to sing,
"Fiddle-de-dee!
Come, foxy, and see
How gay we can be."

The fox had five children.

They heard the cat sing.

One of the children
went out to see who
was singing.

The cat caught her
and put her in his bag.

1. Why did the cat cry?
2. What did the cat
take to the fox's house?
3. What did he do there?

Then the cat sang again,
"Fiddle-de-dee! Fiddle-de-dee!
Come, foxy, and see
How gay we can be."

Another one
of the fox's children
came out to hear him sing.

The cat caught her
and put her in his bag.
Then he sang again
and caught the other children.

He took them home
and shut them up.

1. How did the cat
get the fox's other children?
2. How many were in the bag?
3. Where did he take the bag?

The fox went to look
for his children.

He looked and looked.
Soon he came
to the cat's house.

He said to the cat,
"Where are my children?"

The cat said,
"I have all of your children
in my house.
But you must bring
the cock back to me.
Then I will
let your children go.
But you must never
come near our house again."

1. How did the cat get the cock back?

2. How did the fox get his children back?

3. What do you think of the cat's trick?

4. What do you think of the fox?

5. What do you think of the cat?

6. What do you think of the cock?

7. Which one would you choose for a friend?

MAKING OTHERS HAPPY

What was the story
we played for the children
in the kindergarten?

Let us now play "The Cat,
the Cock, and the Fox" for them.

Who will choose
some good players?

How many do we need?

This is a very long story.

So we are going to play it
in five parts.

Part 1

Why did the cat
and the cock build a house
in the woods?

Play this part of the story.

Part 2

How did the cock get caught?
Play this part of the story.

Part 3

How did the cock get caught the next time?
Play this part of the story.

Part 4

What did the cat do when she got home?
What did she do then?
Play this part of the story.

Part 5

How did the fox get back his children?
Play this part of the story.

To-morrow we will play all of the story.

THE HOUSE IN THE WOODS

Do you remember the house
that the cat and the cock
built in the woods?

Let us play that we
are cats and cocks.

Let us build a house
on the board.

---

1. Who will draw the walls
and the roof?

2. Who will make a place
for Santa Claus
to get into the house?

3. Who will make a door?

4. Who will draw
three windows?

5. Who can make smoke
come out of the chimney?

HOW THE FOX PLAYED HERDSMAN

Once upon a time,
a dear old woman
lived all alone on a farm.

She had some cows, some sheep, some pigs, and some chickens.

She went to market
every day.

So she could not watch
her cows and sheep and pigs.

She said,
"I must have a herdsman."

So she started out
to look for a herdsman.

SHE MEETS A BEAR

Very soon she met a bear.

"Where are you going?"
asked the bear.

"I am looking for a herdsman," said the dear old woman.

"Well," said Mr. Bear, "why don't you take me?"

"Can you call the cows and the sheep and the pigs?" asked the dear old woman.

"Just hear me call," said Mr. Bear.

And he called, "Grr— —, Grr— —."

"No, no, you will not do. Your voice is too cross," said the dear old woman.

Then she went on.

SHE MEETS A WOLF

Soon she met a wolf.

"Where are you going?" asked Mr. Wolf.

"I am looking for a herdsman," said the dear old woman.

"Well," said Mr. Wolf, "why don't you take me?"

"Can you call the cows and the sheep and the pigs?" asked the dear old woman.

"Listen," said Mr. Wolf. And he called, "Woof--, Woof--."

"No, no, you will not do. Your voice is too cross," said the dear old woman.

Then she went on.

SHE MEETS A FOX

By and by she met a fox.

"Where are you going?" asked Mr. Fox.

"I am looking for a herdsman," said the dear old woman.

"Well," said Mr. Fox, "why don't you take me?"

"Can you call the cows
and the sheep and the pigs?"
asked the dear old woman.

"Just hear me call,"
said Mr. Fox.

And he called,
"Purr— —, Purr— —."

"Your voice is just right
for a good herdsman,"
said the dear old woman.

"Come home with me,
and you can watch the cows
and the sheep and the pigs."

1. Why did the dear old woman need a herdsman?
2. How many animals did she meet?
3. Whom did she meet first?
4. Why didn't she choose him?
5. Whom did she meet next?
6. Why didn't she choose him?
7. Whom did she meet last?
8. Why did she choose him?

So, every morning,
the fox drove the cows
and the sheep and the pigs
to pasture.

And every evening,
he brought them back.

But, one day,
the dear old woman
counted the cows and the sheep
and the pigs.

One of the cows
had not come back.

So she asked Mr. Fox,
"Where is the old red cow?"

"I will look in the woods
for her to-morrow,"
said Mr. Fox.

The next day,
the dear old woman
asked Mr. Fox,
"Where is
the little black pig?"
"He ran away from me,"
said Mr. Fox.
"I will look for him
to-morrow."
The next day,
the dear old woman
asked Mr. Fox,
"Where is
the big black sheep?"
"He went to the brook
to get a drink,"
said Mr. Fox.
"I will look for him
to-morrow."

That night, the dear old woman was making some bread.

She watched Mr. Fox when he brought back the cows and the sheep and the pigs.

She thought that some more of her cows had not come back.

THE FOX IS CAUGHT

The fox shut the cows and the sheep in the barn.

He shut the pigs in their pen.

Then he walked through the yard where the chickens lived.

He did not see the dear old woman.

So he took a big, fat hen, and put her in his bag.

The dear old woman
saw the fox
take the hen.

So she ran after him.

She caught him by the tip of his tail, but he pulled away.

She had flour on her hands, and some of it was left on the tip of Mr. Fox's tail.

There it is to-day.

And that is why the tip of a fox's tail is always white.

1. Why did the dear old woman watch the fox?
2. What did she see him do?
3. What did she do then?
4. How did the flour get on the dear old woman's hands?
5. How does the story end?
6. Can you think of another end for this story?

OLD FRIENDS

Here is a list of old friends.

You made these friends in other books.

How many of them do you remember?

a	at	boy
after	ate	but
again	away	by
all		
am	baby	call
an	back	came
and	be	can
any	bed	cat
apple	big	children
are	bird	cold
as	blue	come

could
cow

day
did
do
does
dog
down

eat

father
fire
flew
flowers
fly
for
found
from

gave
get
girl
give
go
goes
going
good
green
grow

had
hand
has
have
he
hear
help
hen
her
here
hill
him
his
home
horse
house
how

I
if
in
into
is
it

know

let
like

little
live
look

made
make
man
may
me
might
mouse
morning
mother
much
must
my

near
never

no
not
now

of
Oh
old
on
one
or
our
out
over

pig
play
please
put

rabbit
ran
red
run

said
sat
say
says
saw
see
shall
she
should
sing
snow
so
some
soon
sun

take
tell
that
the
them
then
there
they
think
this
three
time
to
too

tree
two

under
up
us

want
was
water
we
well
went
were

what
when
where
white
who
why
will
winter
with
would

yes
you
your

NEW FRIENDS

Here is a list of new friends.

How many
do you remember?

The numbers tell the pages
where you can find
your new friends.

If you can not remember a
friend, turn back to the page.

Read the page again.

Then you will remember
your new friend.

2	3
Polly	arm
cracker	book
heard	4
parrot	Moo-moo
talk	Quack-quack

Bow-wow
Peep-peep
Meow-meow

5

rooster
duck
chick
goose
owl
turkey
sheep

6

standing
street
selling
something
many
round
held
strings
colors
yellow
once
sky

7

making
balloons
teacher
paper
find
crayon
hold
draw
desk

8

black
turn

9

birthday
cake

stand
wish
happy

10
blackboard
candles
need
more
these

11
light
blow

12
playing
doing

13
name
toys
happened
train
dolls
soldiers
read
about
lead

14
box
march
world
raise

15
meets
rag
halt
stood
still

16
friend
every
both
whom
first
ask

18
next
remember
part
story
perhaps

19
woolly

20
choose
begin

21
lion

22
roared
fight
very
began
tear
torn
pieces

23
act

24
others
kindergarten
players

26
last

27
puzzles
words
left
page

28
sheet
thin
trace
four
row

29
write
number
cut

30
sparrow
blade
grass
swing

31
off
goat
Mr.
because
answered

32
flies
wolf

34
easy

36
burn

38
ox
drink

39
terrible
fright

40
Hush-a-bye
top
better
tight
drop

41
finding
wet
which
animals

42
dressing

43
middle
hair
stockings
brown
right

44
their
corner
jumped
candlestick
sleep
haystack

45
pieman
lost
cupboard
tuffet
ready
pencil

46
Fairy
Health

writing
letter

47

dear
strong
milk
fruit
candy
always
brush
teeth
early
open
windows
love

48

try

49

things
send

orange
banana

50

tea
party
set
table
cup
mine
saucers

51

sugar
bowl
empty
cream
care
kitchen
surprise
eyes
hard

baked
Gingerbread

52

invited

53

rains
people

54

truck
along
brave

55

policeman
obey

56

bag
mailman
ever

bring
wrote

57

silently
walk

58

bread
burning
cross
coal
ice
ashes

59

radio
Bears
story-teller
listen
ears

60
chairs

61
upstairs
end

62
Goldenhair
rap
door
porridge

63
movies
buy
tickets

64
theater
outside

65
best

66
sell
seats

67
sentences
yourself
barked
drove

68
pets
hop
wings

69
feeding
food
five

70
woman
Mrs.

garden
lettuce
cabbage
carrots

71
throw
stone

72
threw

77
smiled
stop

80
paints
each

81
week
Sunday
Monday
Tuesday
Wednesday
Thursday
Friday
Saturday
before

82
yesterday
to-morrow

83
school

84
stories

85
windy
football
Santa Claus

86
sea
shore
season

87
ladies
ponies
riding
else

88
year
spring
summer
fall
new
leaves
plant
weather
warm
bloom

89
nuts
ripe
Jack Frost
South

92
kite
pulling
sled

93
body
head
nose
mouth
melt

94
Fred
Flo
took

piles
great
worked
funny

95
thought
shine
alas
pass

96
Gray Mouse
cheese
frightened

97
Long Nose
Sharp Ears
afraid
noise
claws

98
smell
mice
plan
tie
neck

102
matter

104
together

106
fairies
another
manners

107
waves
wand

108
questions
answers
front

109
lady
older
room

110
basket

111
Grandmother
saved

112
using
telephone
Central
wrong
line

115
busy

116
family

117
meal
speaking
sent

118
flag

119
salute
stripes
large

120
game
taps

121
soft
feet
short

122
farm
scolded
crow
loudly

123
built
build

124
caught
sly
dinner
sang
cried
pussy

125
alone

126
corn

127
stay

128
trick
fiddle

129
Fiddle-de-dee
foxy
gay

130
shut

135
roof
place

smoke
chimney

136
herdsman
chickens
market
watch

137
started

138
voice

140
Woof

142
Purr

143
pasture
brought
counted

144
brook

146
barn
pen
through
yard

148
tip
pulled
flour